TOO MUCH TALK

WRITTEN BY

Angela Shelf Medearis

ILLUSTRATED BY

Stefano Vitale

WALKER BOOKS

AND SUBSIDIARIES

LONDON · BOSTON · SYDNEY

One day a farmer in West Africa
went out to gather some yams.

While he was digging, a yam said to him, "You did not water me. You did not weed me. And here you come to dig me up!"

"Well!" said the farmer. First he looked around. Then he looked at his dog and said, "Were you talking to me?"

"No," barked the dog. "It was the yam."

"Aiyeee!" screamed the farmer. He ran and he ran, uphill and downhill. And he ran and he ran, downhill and uphill. He ran until he met a man who was carrying some fish.

"Why are you running in the heat of the day?" said the fisherman.

"Well," said the farmer, "first my yam talked and then my dog talked!"

"Oh," said the fisherman, "that can't happen."

"Oh, yes it can," the fish said to them. "Aiyeee!" screamed the farmer and the fisherman. They ran and they ran, uphill and downhill. And they ran and they ran, downhill and uphill. They ran until they met a man who was weaving some cloth.

"Why are you running in the heat of the day?" the weaver said.

"Well," said the farmer, "first my yam talked, then my dog talked, and then the fish talked."

"Oh," said the weaver, "that can't happen."

"Oh, yes it can," the cloth said to them.
"Aiyeee!" screamed the farmer and the fisherman and the weaver. They ran and they ran, uphill and downhill. And they ran and they ran, downhill and uphill. They ran until they came to a woman who was swimming.

"Ahhhh," said the swimmer as she glided through the water. "Why are you running in the heat of the day?"

"Well," said the farmer, "first my yam talked, then my dog talked, then the fish talked, and then the cloth talked."

"Oh," said the swimmer as she did the backstroke, "that can't happen."

"Oh, yes it can," the water said to her. "Aiyeee!" screamed the farmer and the fisherman, the weaver and the swimmer. They ran and they ran, uphill and downhill. And they ran and they ran, downhill and uphill. They ran until they came to the house of the chief.

The chief came out and sat on his royal chair. He said to them, "Why are you running in the heat of the day?"

"Well," said the farmer, "first my yam talked, then my dog talked, then the fish talked, then the cloth talked, and then the water talked."

"Talk, talk, talk!" said the chief. "Too much talk! Yams don't talk! Fish don't talk! Cloth doesn't talk! And water doesn't talk! All this foolish talk will disturb the village! Go away, before I throw you in jail!"

So they all ran away.

"Imagine," said the chief, "a talking yam! How can that be?"

"So true," said the chair. "Whoever heard of a talking yam?"

"Aiyeee!" screamed the chief. And he ran uphill and downhill and was never seen again.

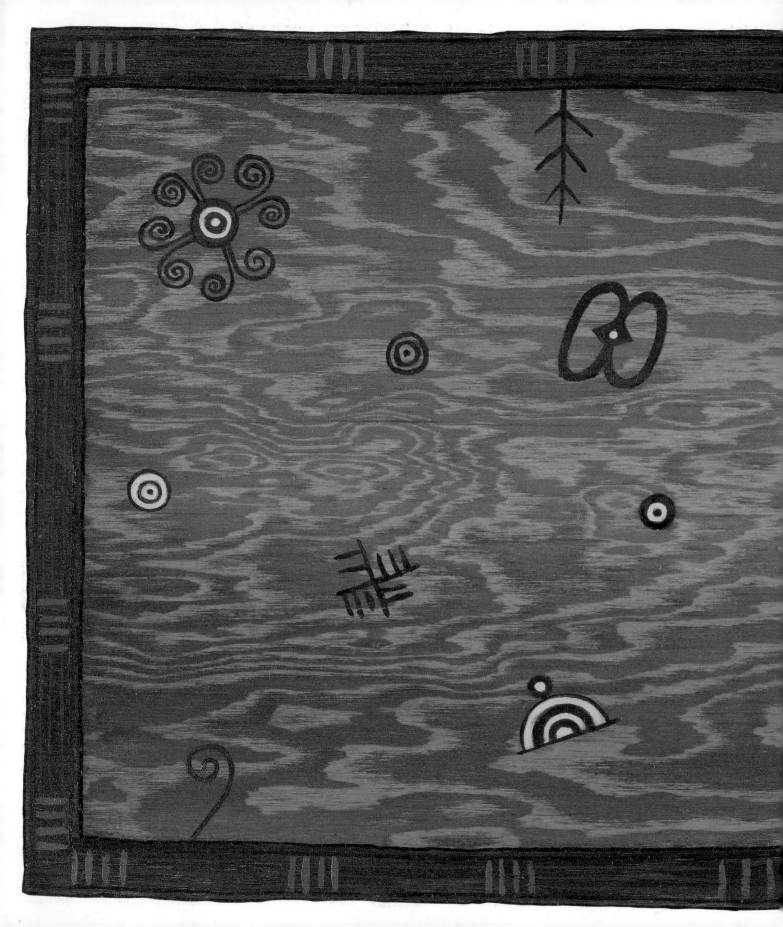

MORE WALKER PAPERBACKS
For You to Enjoy

HANDA'S SURPRISE
by Eileen Browne

As Handa walks a variety of animals help themselves
to the different fruits in the basket on her head.

"Rich in the colours and space of Africa … the pictures are so sensual
the reader can almost smell the various fruits that Handa is carrying…
A delight to read aloud or for beginner readers to read for themselves;
it is beautifully produced and a joy to handle." *The School Librarian*

0-7445-3634-0   £4.99

THE VERY BEST OF AESOP'S FABLES
retold by Margaret Clark/illustrated by Charlotte Voake

Aesop's Fables are among the oldest and best-loved stories in the world.

"Bright as new paint… Clear, snappy and sharp, yet retains all the elegance and
point of the originals. Delicately illustrated by the inimitable Charlotte Voake."
The Sunday Times

0-7445-3149-7   £5.99

LITTLE RABBIT FOO FOO
by Michael Rosen/Arthur Robins

A new version of a popular playground rhyme, in which a naughty biker
bunny gets his come-uppance from The Good Fairy.

"Simple and hilarious… I laugh every time I think about it."
Susan Hill, The Sunday Times

0-7445-2065-7   £4.99